D0677039

Superhero HARRY

The Wild Field Trip

by Rachel Ruiz
illustrated by Steve May

PICTURE WINDOW BOOKS
a capstone imprint

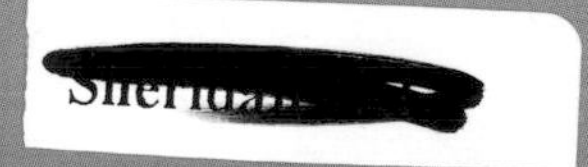

Superhero Harry is published by Picture Window Books
A Capstone Imprint
1710 Roe Crest Drive
North Mankato, Minnesota 56003
www.mycapstone.com

Library of Congress Cataloging-in-Publication Data is available on the Library of Congress website.

ISBN: 978-1-4795-9857-1 (library hardcover)
ISBN: 978-1-4795-9861-8 (paperback)

Designer: Hilary Wacholz

Printed and bound in the USA

010370F17

TABLE OF CONTENTS

ALL ABOUT Superhero HARRY

NAME: Harrison Albert Cruz

FAVORITE COLOR: red

FAVORITE FOOD: spaghetti

FAVORITE SCHOOL SUBJECT: science

HOBBIES: playing video games, inventing, and reading

IDOLS: Albert Einstein and Superman

BEST FRIEND, NEIGHBOR, AND SIDEKICK: Macy

LATEST INVENTION: Super Swinger Wristbands

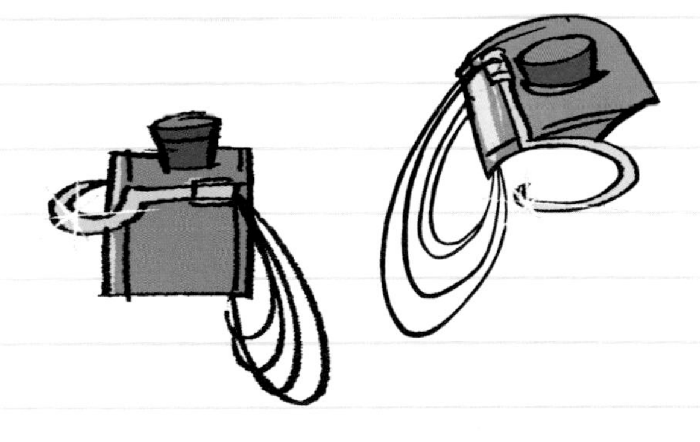

CHAPTER 1

THE LATEST INVENTION

Harry's school bus will be here any minute. He should be getting ready for the zoo field trip. Instead he's finishing up his latest superhero invention.

Harry LOVES superheroes. He wishes he had superpowers. But he's just a normal kid.

Harry builds inventions to make him more like a superhero. Harry's inventions don't always work. But he never stops trying.

Once he invented supersonic headphones. He used earmuffs, two empty soup cans, and a long string. The string was so long, Harry got tangled up in it and fell down.

Another time Harry made super stilt legs to help him reach things. He used what he thought were empty coffee cans and an old bungee cord.

But the coffee cans were not empty. Harry left a trail of coffee from the kitchen to his room. His dad was not happy.

Harry's latest invention was perfect for the class field trip to the zoo. He had been working on the it for weeks!

Harry's favorite animals are monkeys. And monkeys swing from branch to branch. So Harry built an invention that will help him be a super swinger just like a monkey!

Harry made wristbands with a button in the center of each. When he presses the button, wires shoot out. Each wristband has one wire.

The wires have coat hanger hooks attached to their ends. The hooks should grab onto tree branches.

Once the hooks attach, Harry will be able to swing like a monkey. At least that's how Harry hopes they will work.

"Harry!" his mom calls. "The bus is here!"

"Coming!" Harry says.

CHAPTER 2

SUPER SWINGER WRISTBANDS

"Over here, Harry!" says Macy.

Macy is Harry's next-door neighbor, superhero sidekick, classmate, and best friend. She always saves him a seat on the bus. Harry sits down next to her.

"What are those?" Macy asks, looking at the wristbands.

"My latest invention," Harry says proudly. "I call them the super swinger wristbands."

"How do they work?" Macy asks.

Harry explains his latest invention to Macy.

"So you've tested them out already?" she asks.

"Not yet," Harry says. "But I know they'll work."

"I don't know, Harry," Macy says.

But Harry says, "Trust me."

When they arrive at the zoo, Harry's class visits the giraffes first.

Jason stands on his tiptoes and stretches his neck to try and look like a giraffe.

Next they visit the penguins.

"Look at those cute little guys!" Macy says. "They look like they're wearing tuxedos!"

As the penguins waddle around, Ethan and Jackson pin their arms to their sides and waddle like penguins.

Then they go to the bird habitat. Harry looks at the birds flying up above.

"Next time I'll invent super flying wristbands. Then I can fly with the birds," Harry says.

"What are those?" Violet asks, pointing at Harry's wristbands.

"Are we talking about Harry's super swinging wristbands?" asks Macy.

"What are super swinging wristbands?" Melanie asks.

"Harry's latest invention," Macy says.

"How do they work, Harry?" Jackson asks.

"You'll see when we get to the monkeys, right Harry?" Macy says.

"That's right," Harry says. "Be prepared. Something really amazing is going to happen!"

CHAPTER 3

MR. BUNNY BUNNY

After lunch, the moment Harry has been waiting for finally arrives.

"All right, second graders," Ms. Lane says. "The next stop is the primate habitat. Everyone stay together."

Harry is so excited. He looks around and sees a lot of good trees for swinging. He decides it's time to test out his latest invention.

But Harry gets distracted when he hears a little girl crying.

She keeps saying, "Mr. Bunny Bunny! Mr. Bunny Bunny!"

She's pointing to her stuffed bunny. It's on the other side of the fence. Her dad is busy talking to another adult. He doesn't even notice!

"She must have thrown it over," Harry says quietly. "This seems like a job for Superhero Harry. After all, superheroes should save the day!"

The stuffed bunny isn't too far from the fence. Harry tries to grab it. But his arm is too big to fit under the fence.

Next, he finds a long tree branch. He tries to sweep the stuffed bunny toward the fence. But that doesn't work either.

"Wait a minute," Harry says. "My super swinging wristbands will be perfect for this!"

Harry pushes the button on his right wristband. The wire shoots out. One of the coat hanger hooks grabs Mr. Bunny Bunny.

Harry presses the button again to make the wire come back. Mr. Bunny Bunny flies right over the fence!

Once Mr. Bunny Bunny is safely in his arms, he gives it to the little girl.

She gives Mr. Bunny Bunny a big hug. Then she gives Harry a big hug.

Harry can't believe he did it! His invention actually works!

CHAPTER 4

MONKEY MADNESS

"Harry, there you are!" Macy says. "Everyone else already moved ahead."

"You missed it, Macy!" Harry says. "I just saved a little girl's stuffed bunny. I used my cool wristbands and everything. I was a real superhero!"

"Your invention really works?" Macy says. "You have to show me!"

"Get ready, monkeys," Harry says. "Here I come!"

Harry aims one wristband at the closest tree. He pushes the button. Nothing happens. He pushes the button again. Still, nothing happens.

"You said it worked," Macy says.

"It does!" Harry says. "Let me try it one more time. It might just be stuck."

He pushes the button again. This time a wire shoots out. But it doesn't hook onto the tree.

Instead it hooks around a little monkey's leg!

Without thinking, Harry pushes the button again. The scared little monkey comes flying over the fence. It safely lands in a small bush. At the same time, the wire on Harry's wristband breaks.

"This is bad," Harry says. "Real bad."

"What are we going to do?" Macy asks.

"We have to fix this," Harry says. "And we have to do it fast."

"How?" Macy asks.

"Just follow me," Harry says.

CHAPTER 5

THE BANANA

Harry runs over to the little monkey. Macy is close behind him. The monkey is all tangled up in the wire and the bush.

Harry quickly untangles the monkey. Then he gives him a banana. The little monkey doesn't look scared anymore.

“Do you always carry around a banana?” Macy asks.

“I do when I’m going to the zoo,” Harry says. “You never know when you might need it.”

“Now what do we do?” Macy asks.

"We swing," Harry says.

"I have no idea what you are talking about," Macy says.

"Just watch," Harry says.

He takes off the broken wristband. He climbs on a bench and carefully holds the monkey.

Harry pushes the button on his left wristband. The wire shoots out. It misses the tree. Harry tries again. It misses again.

"I don't think this is going to work," Macy says.

"It will work! Third time is a charm!" Harry says.

This time the wire hits the tree. It sticks to the branch! Harry and the monkey fly over the fence, swinging from the tree.

"You did it!" Macy yells.

The monkey climbs onto the branch. Harry climbs onto the branch too. Now Harry just needs to get out.

Harry takes the hook from the super swinger out of the tree. He pulls the wire back into his wristband. Harry aims it at a tree on the other side of the fence.

He takes a deep breath and pushes the button. It grips on the first time!

"Hurry, Harry!" Macy yells.

Harry jumps and swings to safety. As he swings, Harry gets all tangled up in the wire. His landing is a mess, but he did it.

His invention really works!

"That was so cool," Macy says. "And now we have to hurry. The bus is here!"

"Roger that," Harry says.

Macy helps Harry untangle the wire. Macy is extra good at it since she is always untangling her necklaces.

"Come on, Harry! We are going to miss the bus!" Macy yells.

Harry and Macy run through the zoo. They pass the giraffes. They pass the lions. They pass the penguins.

"I wish you had invented something to make us fly," Macy says. "That would be really handy right now!"

"I'm working on it," Harry says, huffing and puffing. "One invention at a time."

They get to the bus, quietly climb on, and sit down. Ms. Lane looks suspicious but doesn't say anything.

"Now that we have everyone we can head back," Ms. Lane tells the bus driver.

"This was one wild field trip," Macy says.

"It sure was! I can't wait to get started on my next superhero invention," Harry says.

"What are you going to make next?" Macy asks.

"I'm not sure, but I know it's going to be cool. Superhero Harry, over and out!" he says.

GLOSSARY

bungee cord — a strong rope that can be stretched and has hooks on both ends

field trip — a visit to a place so students can learn about something

habitat — the place or type of place where a plant or animal normally lives or grows

headphones — a device that is worn over your ears and used for listening to music without having other people hear it

invention — a useful new device

primate — any member of the group of animals that includes humans, apes, and monkeys

sidekick — a person who helps and spends a lot of time with someone

supersonic — faster than the speed of sound

tuxedo — a formal black suit worn with a white shirt and a black bow tie

waddle — to walk with short steps while moving from side to side

TALK ABOUT IT

1. Harry's inventions don't always work. But he keeps trying. Talk about a time when you had to keep trying. What happened?

2. Do you think Harry's invention is safe? Why or why not?

3. Do you think Harry should tell his parents what happened at the zoo? Why or why not?

WRITE ABOUT IT

1. Write about a field trip you would like to go on with your class.

2. Pretend you are a reporter. Write an article about Harry and his zoo adventure.

3. Macy is Harry's best friend. Make a list of ways Macy supports Harry.

ABOUT THE AUTHOR

Rachel Ruiz is the author of several children's books. She was inspired to write her first book picture book, When Penny met POTUS, after working for Barack Obama on his re-election campaign in 2012.

When Rachel isn't writing books, she writes and produces TV shows and documentaries. She lives in her hometown of Chicago with her husband and their daughter.

ABOUT THE ILLUSTRATOR

Steve May is a professional illustrator and animation director. He says he spent his childhood drawing lots of things and discovering interesting ways of injuring himself.

Steve's work has become a regular feature in the world of children's books. He still draws lots but injures himself less regularly now. He lives in glamorous north London, and his mom says he's a genius.

BE A SUPERHERO AND READ THEM ALL!

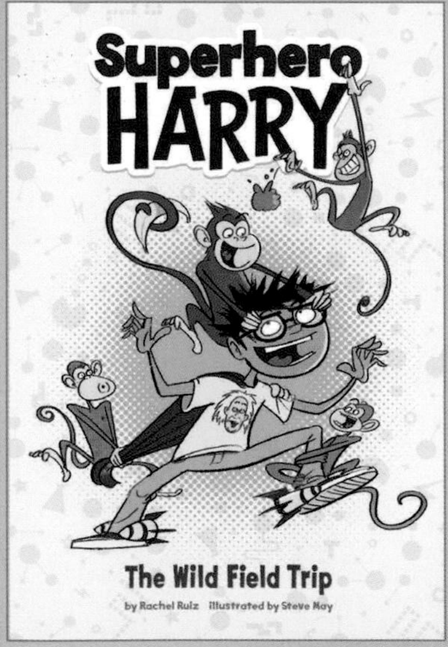